Hans rescues Anna when she falls into a boat!

Anna dances with Hans at the coronation party.

Elsa does not approve of Anna's love for Hans.

Elsa is hiding a secret! The secret comes out
when Anna takes off one of Elsa's gloves.

Elsa can freeze things with her bare hands.

Anna leaves Arendelle to find her sister. She asks Hans
to watch over the kingdom.

Anna rides her horse into the mountains. She will do anything to bring Elsa home!

A cold Anna decides to warm up at a nearby trading post.

The trading post belongs to a *really* big man named Oaken.

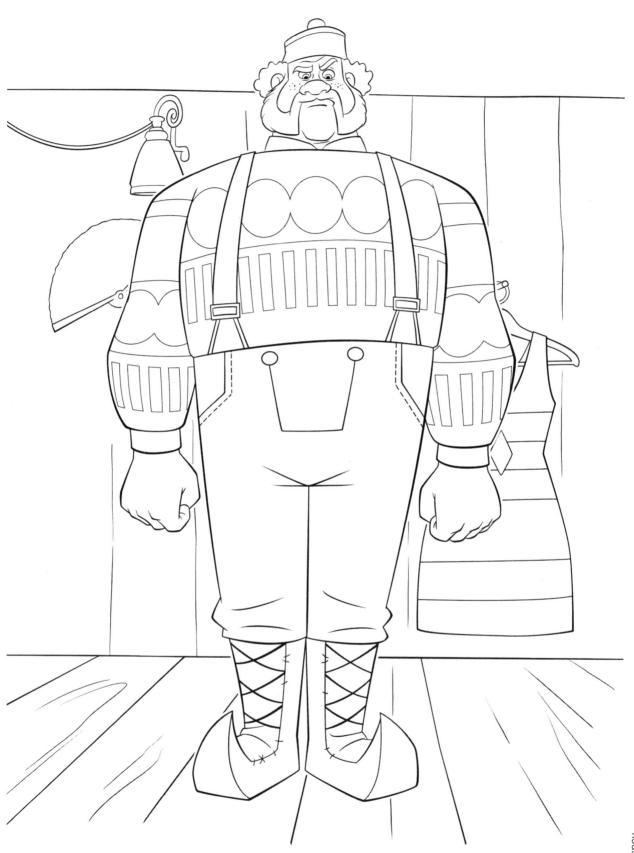

Kristoff is a mountain climber who likes to travel alone—
except for his reindeer, Sven!

Sven loves eating carrots!

Anna brings supplies to Kristoff and Sven.
They have agreed to help her find Elsa.

Olaf is a friendly snowman Elsa made with her magical powers.

Anna remembers Olaf from her childhood.
She is surprised to see him!

Everything is sparkly and beautiful in Elsa's winter wonderland!

Sven wants to eat Olaf's carrot nose! Olaf thinks Sven
wants to be his friend.

Hans is concerned when Anna's horse returns to Arendelle alone.
He sets out to find her.

Finally free to use her magical powers, Elsa begins a new life.

Elsa's ice palace sits on a mountaintop.

Elsa becomes the Snow Queen.

Anna asks Elsa to return home.

Elsa refuses to go back to her old life. Anna doesn't know what to do!

Elsa blasts Anna with ice, accidentally putting a freezing curse on her!

Kristoff wants to help Anna.

Olaf meets a giant snowman and names him Marshmallow.

Marshmallow chases Anna and Kristoff through the forest!

Anna and Kristoff escape from Marshmallow by jumping over a cliff.

Oh, no! Anna is starting to freeze because of Elsa's magic.

Kristoff hurries to get Anna to the trolls.
The magical creatures will know how to save her.

A wise troll tells Anna that only an act of true love
will stop her from freezing.

Kristoff and Anna ride Sven back to Arendelle.
They must find a way to break the curse!

Elsa just wants to be left alone.

Elsa tries to run away.

Anna is sad to leave Kristoff.

Hans brings Elsa back to Arendelle.
Elsa wants to help her sister before it's too late!

Anna needs an act of true love to break the curse,
but Hans won't kiss her.

Hans reveals that he really wants Anna and Elsa out of his way.

Time is running out for Anna to break the curse!

Hans lies about Elsa and Anna so that
he can become King of Arendelle.

Sven senses that something is wrong.
He wants to turn back toward Arendelle.

Olaf sees Kristoff and Sven in the distance!

Anna and Olaf need to escape from the castle!

Anna is almost completely frozen.

Anna needs an act of true love—and soon!

Hans sees Elsa in the snow.

Hans tries to attack Elsa, but Anna stops him.

Saving Elsa was an act of true love. The curse is broken!

Elsa and Anna return to their true selves, as sisters forever.

Elsa can now control her magic and bring back summer.

Elsa, Anna, and Kristoff are happy that summer
has returned to Arendelle.

Elsa keeps the air around Olaf cold so
he can enjoy a warm, sunny day.

Anna takes supplies to Kristoff and Sven in the mountains.

Anna surprises Kristoff with a kiss!

Elsa uses her powers to make an indoor ice-skating rink!

Elsa and Anna might be very different,
but they still love each other very much!